Coming soon!!!
Pronounced "Q"

DC BOOK **DIVA** PRESENTS

DUTCH

PART 1
FEBRUARY 1989

"Yo, B, I'm sayin' (sniff) we eatin' (sniff-sniff) but we ain't eatin' eatin'… you know what I'm sayin', B?" YaYa said between sniffs of heroin. He held the wax paper carefully between his heavily jeweled fingers, using his pinkie nail to powder his nose. "Now Fell and them? They out West Virginia gettin' they weight up."

"I hear you, B," Shameeq replied, smoking a blunt and pushing his cocaine white kitted Benz 190 down Market Street.

"And not only Fell," YaYa added, "Beeb and them down South, Fu Ak up in Connecticut, Mel Kwon out in Ohio… I'm tellin' you, B, we need to migrate! Get the fuck up outta Newark and fuckin' feast," YaYa emphasized, thumbing his nose as he sat back in the plush piped interior and lit a cigarette.

Shameeq looked over at his man, shearling coated up and truck jewelry'd down, looking like a dark skin version of Rakim. If it wasn't for the system banging out the truck, every time YaYa moved it would've sounded like slave chains clanking together. He had on that much jewelry. They were barely twenty and already heavy hitters.

Shameeq handed him the blunt, chuckling. "We ain't eatin'. How you sound, B? Avon doin' five of them things a week, 17th Ave doin' eight on a bad week, not to mention—"

"I ain't say we wasn't eatin'. I said we wasn't EATIN' EATIN'," YaYa replied, eyelids getting droopy.

Shameeq sucked his teeth like 'stop playin'. Word is bond, Ya, if you was stackin' yo' shit instead of putting it around your neck and up your nose, you'd be EATIN' EATIN', B," Shameeq argued, even though he was damn near as jeweled up as YaYa.

1

"Fuck that, B, I'm a muhfuckin' Don," YaYa replied, going into a dope lean

"Whatever, B."

Shameeq pulled over and double parked in front of Ali's jewelry store to pick up the nugget bracelet Ali was fixing for him. He threw on the hazard lights and hopped out into the frigid early morning air.

Downtown Newark on a Saturday seemed to stay crowded, even in the coldest weather. Shameeq was on his way in the store when a brand new burgundy Acura Legend Coupe at the light caught his eye. The system was pumping "Like This" so loud, it even drowned out Shameeq's system sitting only a few feet away. His eyes followed the car as it made a left on Halsey Street. He got a glance at the driver and his eyes got big as plates.

"Oh shit!" he cursed, jogging back to the car. He snatched the door open and got in so quick his entrance made YaYa snap out of his dope nod and snatch the pistol from his waist.

"Meeq, the fuck wrong wit' you?" YaYa growled, mad he disturbed his nod.

Shameeq threw the car in drive and pulled out, making a right on Halsey in pursuit of the coupe.

"I just seen KG bitch ass," Shameeq gritted.

"From Elizabeth?"

"I know this muhfucka ain't buy no new whip wit' my paper," Shameeq growled. He had to run the next light to keep up with the Acura. By the time they reached the end of Halsey, Shameeq flashed his lights until the Acura pulled over. Both cars double parked then Shameeq hopped out and stepped up to the driver's side window as KG lowered it.

"Sha—"

"Yo, B, this you?" Shameeq asked angrily. He had already peeped the temporary license in the back window. "Please tell me you ain't buy no new whip!"

KG thought seriously about just pulling off, but the look in Shameeq's eyes seemed to dare him to do just that, while Shameeq's hand rested under his Giants hoodie.

2

"Yo, yo, Sha, word to mother, I was comin' to see you. I just been—" KG tried to explain, talking so fast the words tumbled out over each other.

Shameeq opened the door. "Get out," he told KG calmly. KG hesitated, so Shameeq repeated it more firmly. "Yo! Get the fuck out!"

KG got out slowly, watching Shameeq's hands. "Yo, Sha, this word to mother, B, I was coming to see you —"

"When? After you spent my shit up?! I ain't seen you in two months, now all of a sudden you was comin' to see me?!" Shameeq blazed him, getting madder with every word.

KG could see it building in him so he quickened his plea. "I got like two on me now —"

"Two?!" Shameeq echoed, spit flying out of his mouth and lightly sprinkling KG's face.

"Two?!" You owe me seventeen, niggah, not two!!"

"I... I know."

"You tryin' to play me, B?!"

"No, 'Meeq, never that—"

"Huh?!"

"Sha, word to mother!"

"Fuck your mother, gimme the keys," Shameeq demanded, looking around, scanning for the police.

"Sha, man, I swear I'ma—"

Smack!

Shameeq cut off KG's weak pleas by smacking the shit out of him.

"Yo, B, chill!" KG hollered, holding his face.

"You think I'm fuckin' playin?!" Shameeq hissed, hooking KG with a vicious left that crumpled him against the trunk of the car. He stood KG up and went in his pockets. "Punk muhfucka, you gonna disrespect me like that, huh?! You think shit is sweet?! Shut up, don't say shit, you disgust me," Shameeq barked while he beat KG ass, pocketing KG's money.

"Yo, Sha, you dead wrong for that, Ock," YaYa yelled from the car laughing.

"Come on, Shameeq man, don't do it like that. I swear I'ma get yo' money, yo," KG mumbled as his lip swelled.

3

Shameeq smirked like, "Then get it. But until then... the 'Ack me, B." He shoved KG off the car and got in under the wheel. It was then that he realized there was a chick in the car. He looked at her as he closed the door.

"Yo, your man owed me money. You part of the payment or something?"

She sucked her teeth like, "Picture that."

"Then get the fuck out!"

"Hmph! And freeze? Please... somebody takin' me home," she sassed then crossed her arms over her breasts.

Shameeq looked shortie over. She was a fly chinky eyed cinnamon bun with mad attitude. Her hair was cut like Anita Baker and she wore two sets of bamboo earrings. One pair had her name across it.

"Okay, Nikki," Shameeq shrugged, reading her earrings. He pulled off watching KG standing in the street behind him.

"Whatever... Drama," she replied, smirking.

He looked at her. "Yo, who is Drama?" he asked, playing stupid.

Everybody in the streets called him Drama except his crew. He would answer to it, but he never called himself by it.

"Who don't know Drama?" she replied, adding in her mind, *wit' your fine ass.* She was holding her composure, but on the inside, her stomach was doing back flips and semis. With his Egyptian bronze skin tone, hazel eyes, wavy hair and dimples, every ghetto chick wanted his type of Drama in their lives. He was 6'1", bow-legged and his swagger gave chicks chills.

"So you fuck wit' clowns like that?" he asked, looking through KG tape collection.

"No," she answered quickly.

"I can't tell. All them bags back there. Sh... you must be one of them bitches that juice nigguhs, huh?" he said, popping in 3XDope's "Funky Dividends."

"Like I need a man to take care of me," she replied dismissively, "all that's for his son which he too sorry to provide for. Shit, the only reason he in town is 'cause I threatened to take his ass to court," she explained.

4

"In town? Where he was at?" Shameeq's ears perked up.

"Virginia."

"Doing what?"

"What you think?"

Shameeq's mind went back to what YaYa was talking about earlier.

"That's why you nor I seen him. He owed me too," Nikki chuckled.

Shameeq looked at Nikki. She was a dime, no question, but she ran her mouth and had no loyalty to a man she had a child with. Still he could tell she was open on him, so he planned on making fucking KG's baby mama part of KG's payment. But first he had to fuck with her head.

"Where you live?" he asked.

"Brick Towers."

At the next block he pulled over in front of the bus stop. She looked at him confusedly.

"What? You thought I was takin' you home? Picture that. I got shit to do," he said, holding in a smirk.

"Like you can't take me a few more blocks, Drama. Brick Towers ain't that far," she snapped.

"Yeah well, I ain't goin' that way," he answered, looking at his Movado, then glanced in the rearview. "Here comes the bus now. You betta hurry up."

She eyed him to see if he was serious then sucked her teeth. She reached in the back for the bags but Shameeq stopped her.

"What you doin', yo? Didn't I tell you he owed me doe?"

"What my baby's clothes got to do wit' that?" Nikki probed.

"Like I ain't got a son," Shameeq lied, but she kept reaching. He jerked her arm like, "Fuck you deaf? That shit mine. Now beat it, your bus is coming," he said, bopping his head to the music.

Nikki was close to tears. "That's foul, Drama, word is bond, that's foul," she said, but Shameeq turned up the radio rapping along with E.S.T.

Nikki got out. She pulled her earmuffs out of her pocket and put them on her ears. Shameeq pulled off then headed straight for

5

the bus stop on the corner of Elizabeth and High Street, where he knew she'd get off. He knew with her good looks, she was used to dudes fawning over her every whim. So he decided to put down the demonstration so she knew it was all about him, not her.

A few minutes later, the bus pulled up and Nikki got off. Shameeq blew the horn then pulled up beside her.

Nikki rolled her eyes and kept walking. Shameeq lowered the passenger window, smiling. "Ay, yo, Nikki, my fault, yo. I ain't mean to flip on you like that. I was just mad at your man."

She ignored him and kept walking, so he rolled at a creep beside her.

"Come on, get in. I know it's cold out there," he said, holding back his laughter.

"I'm fine," she replied, but he could damn near hear her teeth chattering.

"At least come get yo' baby's clothes," he offered.

"Keep it."

He slammed on the brakes and barked, "Ay yo, Nikki, bring yo' ass here! I ain't tryin' to have all that attitude, word up! I said I apologize 'cause I like you, but if it's like that, fuck it then!"

Nikki's ears perked up when he told her he liked her, so when Shameeq began to pull off, Nikki called out, "Drama! Hold up!" She pranced over to the car and got in.

"So this mean you accept my apology?" He grinned.

She gave him the eyes like, "Maybe... and like I told you, he ain't my man!!"

Fifteen minutes later, Shameeq was nine inches deep in Nikki's guts. She straddled him as he reclined on the couch, riding him like a thoroughbred. Her firm C cup sized breasts bounced with every stroke, the gushy sounds of sloppy sex filled the room punctuated by her screams of passion.

"Yeeessss, Drama, ohhh right there! Fuck this pussy." She moaned, grinding her hips into him and biting her bottom lip.

Shameeq grabbed her around the back then laid her on the floor. He cocked her legs over his shoulders then started long dicking her like he was trying to knock the bottom out.

6

"Drama, unnnoooo," she gasped, clawing at the floor trying to squirm away from the dick, but she was pinned beneath him helplessly.

"Ahhhh, baby, I-I feel it in m-m-my stomach," she squealed, eyes rolled up in the back of her head.

"Take this dick, bitch," he growled, "tell me you want Drama in your life!" Shameeq slid in as deep as he could go, grinding her spot until her body shook with her fourth orgasm.

"Oh I doooo, I do, I do, I want Drama in my life! I wanna have your baby," she moaned.

Picture that, he thought, being careful not to bust the condom. Shortie definitely had the type of pussy that would make a man rush home, but she played herself by giving it up too quick.

Shameeq fucked her three more times then fell asleep. Shortie woke him up, washed him, fed him and fucked him once more. She wanted him to know the pussy was his when he wanted it. He already knew that because his dick game was crazy.

By the time he left, it was after nine that night. He drove around to his spot on Avon, laughing with his workers about the whole incident with KG and his baby moms. But little did he know the joke would soon be on him.

A black Monte Carlo SS had been sitting in the cut waiting for him to come through. They knew his crew was too deep to try anything right then, so they waited. They had been paid to do the job right. They followed him to YaYa's block on 17th Avenue, but couldn't make their move. Once he left YaYa and hit Irving Turner Boulevard, they finally got their chance.

He pulled up to the light pumping "Ain't No Half-Steppin'" by Big Daddy Kane. The SS pulled up beside him on the passenger side and an Uzi Sub machine gun was stuck out the window. The only thing that saved Shameeq's life was the light turning green and he pulled off a split second before the Uzi began to spit. That split second made all the difference. The shot that burst through the window aimed for his head exploded the headrest, making Shameeq duck and mash the gas.

"What the fuck?!" he barked, but the only answer was a shower of bullets.

7

The staccato sound of the automatic burst filled his ears as he desperately tried to weave in and out of traffic and still stay low. The Acura was fast, but it was no match for the SS. They tried to pull up beside Shameeq, but he veered hard to the right, trying to ram the nose of the SS into a parked car. The screeching sound of metal on metal and shooting sparks danced across the SS head as the driver fought to maintain control. He had the better car but Shameeq had the better driving skills.

Shameeq aimed his Beretta through the back window and opened fire on the SS then he made a hard left, momentarily losing them. The SS came up behind him and bumped the rear. They accelerated trying to push the Acura into the next busy, intersection.

Shameeq turned completely around in the seat and took aim straight at the driver. He shot out the windshield of the SS, causing the driver and shooter to take cover. He used the opportunity to speed up, throw up the emergency break, fish tailing the Acura. That made the SS slam into the rear flank of the Acura and the air bags to explode in the driver and shooter's faces, coming to a screeching halt.

In a second, Shameeq was out of the car and pumping shot after shot at the driver. The air bags exploded on impact and the driver's head jerked back, blood flying everywhere. The passenger, still discombobulated by the accident stumbled out of the passenger door and took off in a drunken sprint. Shameeq let off one more round before his clip was empty.

"Shit!!" he cursed then sprinted off in the opposite direction with the sounds of approaching sirens in the distance.

Not knowing when or what was waiting for him at his crib, Shameeq took a cab up to Vailsburg, where his twin sister Egypt lived. She greeted him at the door with a hug. He peered over her shoulder at the dude sitting on the couch, broke the embrace and said, "Yo, B, you gotta bounce."

"Excuse you?" Egypt quipped, one eyebrow raised.

Shameeq ignored her, grabbed the dude's coat and put it in his lap. "She'll call you later."

"Shameeq!" Egypt bassed.

Dude looked at Shameeq then at Egypt confused.

8

"Yo, B, I'm the one talkin' to you, not her. Family crisis and I ain't tryin' to repeat myself," Shameeq said calmly, but eyed dude firmly.

When Egypt heard him say family crisis, she sighed and said, "Jerome, let me call you later, okay? Let me speak wit' my brother."

There was no denying Shameeq was her brother, because Shameeq and Egypt were the spitting image of one another. Even down to the long eyelashes and thick eyebrows, although Egypt's were slightly arched. She was slim and flat-chested but her hips and ass more than made up the difference. At six feet even and bowlegged just like her brother, the only thing distinctly different was the fact that Egypt wore long skinny salon locs. No extensions, it was all her own hair.

The dude grabbed his coat, like "Yeah aiight." He was eyeing Shameeq hard, but Shameeq had his back to him, talking on Egypt's cordless.

"I'll call you," Egypt whispered, giving dude a kiss on the lips. She closed the door just as Shameeq hung up the phone and sat down.

"Ohhh! This better be good! Bustin' up my groove and I was about to get me some," Egypt fumed with a smirk. She tied two of her dreads around the rest to make a ponytail.

"Watch yo' mouth," Shameeq warned, "Don't make me chase duke down and smash his ass, yo. I'm already heated, don't make it worse."

"Whatever, Shameeq."

"I know whatever. Wait until you get married," he huffed.

"Too late." She giggled, going in the kitchen. "Now what's this crisis or you just here cock blockin'?"

"Muhfuckas tried to kill me."

The sound of silverware hitting the floor was all you heard as Egypt rushed back in the room. "What?! Who?! When?! Are you —" she rattled off, coming over to check his face, but he swatted her hand away.

"I'm ai-ight. Damn mother hen, I said tried."

Egypt stood back with her hands on her hips. "So what we gonna do?"

9

"We? We ain't doin' shit," he replied.

"Oh so you gonna play me lame now? Hell no, Shameeq! You all I got, yo, you think I'm just gonna stand by and let these punk muhfuckas take that?!" She was so vexed, she was close to tears, but she had murder in her heart.

"See, that's why we ain't doin' shit. Look at you 'bout to cry and shit. What you gonna do, huh?" He pointed his fingers like a gun, shaking like he was scared. "You shot at my brother, boo-hoo, I'ma kill you." He chuckled.

"Fuck you, Shameeq," Egypt hissed, and stormed in the kitchen.

"Yeah that's right, you in the best place for a woman," he yelled, although he knew his sister wasn't the average female.

They had grown up parentless since they were eleven, after their mother killed their father then killed herself. She had found him in the bed with another woman. They refused to be split up by the system, so they took to the streets and either hustled or starved.

When crack hit Newark around '85, they used the opportunity to come up. They never looked back. It was him and her against the world, taking the trips to New York, posted up on the corners and handling any beefs that came their way.

When YaYa came home from Caldwell, he and Shameeq took their hammer game to the next level, earning the name Drama Squad, and Shameeq, the name Drama. They stayed in some shit because none of them had a cool head, all three live wires. They were young, black and reckless getting paper and making a name for themselves in the street.

As shit got heated, Shameeq made Egypt fall back, get her G.E.D. then go to Community College, which was where she was then, her second year for business management.

Despite his jokes, Shameeq knew Egypt was serious because she loved her brother to death and she was no stranger to putting in work.

YaYa got there in no time with Trello and Casper. Both were fifteen and hungry to be made in the Drama Squad. Trello was a short brown skin dude that weighed a buck fifty soaking wet, but his Uzi weighed a ton and his hammer game made him a beast.

10

Casper was called that because he was an albino. Red eyes and a deadly temper, he had hands so nice that he was a two time Golden Gloves Champion. He had a promising career awaiting him in the ring but the streets had a hold of him and wouldn't let go.

Shameeq explained the scenario to YaYa and they both came to the same conclusion.

"KG," YaYa surmised.

"I feel like that, too," Shameeq concurred.

"Yo, I told you you was dead wrong, B. You can't play a dude like that in front of his bitch," YaYa said.

"Shameeq, I know this ain't over no pussy," Egypt remarked, knowing her brother. "That shit gonna be the death of you."

"Don't mark me like that, girl. And I told you duke owed me money!"

"But you fucked her though, didn't you?" Egypt inquired, knowing she was right because Shameeq didn't answer.

"Trick."

"Watch yo' mouth."

"But yo, B… yo, it might not be KG," Trello added, "it might be them dudes on Renner still in they feelings 'cause we housed they block."

"Or that kid off 20th Street," Casper added.

"Drama." Egypt smirked, shaking her head at her brother. The streets had named him well.

"So what up? Word to mother B, somebody gotta bleed, rightly or wrongly," YaYa growled, ready to set it.

"Indeed, indeed. So, yo, first thing in the morning we gonna snatch that bitch up!" Shameeq exclaimed.

"What bitch?" Casper asked.

"KG baby moms. If duke did do it, I know exactly how to find out," Shameeq smirked.

The next morning, the Drama Squad waited on the corner of West Kinney and High Street in a brown conversion van, watching for Nikki. She had told Shameeq she worked at the Marriot on 1 & 9. So he knew she'd be coming out any minute. She came out of the building, bundled up in a pink goose parka and match-

11

ing earmuffs. The wind whipped furiously around her as she trekked to the bus stop.

"There she go," Shameeq said from the passenger seat. YaYa pulled off, making a U-turn so he could come up beside her. Nikki didn't notice the van until it was too late. Casper threw the sliding door open then he and Trello jumped out. He cuffed her mouth and snatched her inside the van so fast she didn't have time to scream until she was laying on the back of the van.

"Shut the fuck up!" Shameeq growled, backhanding Nikki. He didn't try to hurt her he just wanted her to know shit was serious.

"Dra-Dra, what did I do?" Nikki sobbed, holding her reddened face.

"You know what you did, bitch! You set me up for your man so he could kill me!" he bassed in her face.

"Noooo! I didn't," Nikki protested, but Shameeq grabbed her by the throat.

"Bitch... don't... lie," he seethed, hazel eyes a crimson red.

"No... I mean... argh," she gagged, "I ... I don't know, no!"

"What you mean you don't know, huh?! You must know somethin' if you know it's somethin' not to know!!" Shameeq grilled her, relaxing the grip on her throat.

"No, Drama, No! I meant I don't know what you're talkin' about! I swear!" she cried, but Shameeq just eyed her without answering. She continued. "K-KG, he called me flippin'... askin' me why I didn't get out wit' him and where you take me."

"And what you tell him?!"

"I told him you dropped me at the bus stop, that's it," she stressed.

Shameeq snorted like, "You expect me to believe that shit?!" he hissed.

"I swear on my mother, Drama!"

"So you sayin' you ain't know he did it?" Shameeq's tone lowered, but he was still skeptical.

"No," she sobbed, "I would never do something like that to you, Drama," she vowed, leaning up and hugging his neck hard. He winked his eye at Casper and Trello then untangled her arms

12

from around his neck. "Naw, yo, I can't trust that shit, yo, I can't trust you!"

"You can, baby, you can trust me," Nikki replied quickly, looking him in the eyes and willing him her heart.

"I can trust you? You sure?"

She nodded then hugged him again.

"Then I need you to do something for me," he began.

Nikki wiped her eyes with the back of her hand and answered like she was down for whatever. "What?"

"I need you to call KG. Don't ask him about shit, just go at him and clown him about me takin' his whip. Ai-ight?" Shameeq instructed her.

"That's it?"

"Yeah."

"What if... what if he did it?" Nikki asked timidly.

"What you think?" he replied, and she could already see KG's blood in his eyes.

"Word is bond Drama, KG ain't much but he all I got. I-I don't care either, but if... who's gonna do for me and my son?" Nikki inquired, hoping this show of loyalty would bond her to him.

He smiled and caressed her face. "You won't have to worry no more, Nikki, I got you," he promised.

She nodded and kissed the palm of his hand. Shameeq and Nikki waited in her apartment. It took awhile for KG to finally call back, after paging him repeatedly. When he did call, Shameeq picked up on the kitchen phone while Nikki had the cordless.

" 'Bout time," Nikki huffed, the sassiness back in her voice, "what? You was fuckin' some bitch?"

"I ain't got time for that shit, Nikki, fuck you want?" KG spat back.

"You ain't got time? I could be callin' 'cause yo' son is sick! What you mean you ain't got time?!" Nikki winked at Shameeq, knowing she was doing her job. He smiled back, but he was thinking, scandalous bitch.

"What... do... you... want?" KG repeated, gritting his teeth.

"I need some money."

"I just took yo'ass shoppin' yester—" KG tried to say.

"And I told you that dude that took your car wouldn't let me get my shit!" she replied.

"Ain't nobody take shit from me! I gave that bitch muhfucka that shit," he exclaimed.

"I can't tell. But anyway, what you gonna do because yo' son still need clothes. It ain't his fault you got stripped." She giggled.

"Bitch, you think that shit cute?! His faggot ass had a gun, that's the only reason I ain't beat his ass! But trust me, after what I sent at his ass last night I bet you he respect KG now!" he boasted, not knowing he had just signed his own death warrant trying to save face with a chick that didn't give a fuck about him.

Shameeq was fuming. He pressed mute on the receiver and whispered, "Get him over here!"

Nikki nodded. "Whatever. Just when you comin'?"

KG sucked his teeth. "I'm 'bout to bounce. I'll wire it to you."

"Oh hell no, Kevin! That's that bullshit! The last time you said that, I ain't get shit. But fuck it I see how you wanna play. Monday morning I will be up in Essex County—"

"You a triflin' bitch, you know that?!" KG spat, "I'll be through there."

"When?"

"Later." He hung up.

"Beep him again," Shameeq ordered. He wanted KG right then.

Nikki did as she was told. She beeped him three times back to back, until KG called back, vexed.

"Bitch, didn't I say later?!" He wanted to strangle Nikki's ass, but he was ready to get back to VA, and he damn sure didn't need a child support warrant hanging over his head.

"And I gotta go to work now! Just come gimme the money so you can go back to your lil' hoes!" she replied.

"Have yo' ass downstairs when I get there. I ain't climbin' all them damn steps!" KG roared then hung up.

"So… what-what you gonna do, Drama?" she asked nervously. "What if he don't come up?"

"He will," he assured her.

"And then?" she probed.

"Nikki."

"Yes?"

"You talk too much. I told you I got you," Shameeq answered, peeping around the curtain like Malcolm X, glock in hand. He could see the front side of Brick Towers, nine stories below. Down the block, YaYa had the van parked.

As they waited, Nikki debated several times whether or not to break the silence. She finally got up the nerve and said, "Drama."

He looked at his watch then at her.

"I... I love you," she blurted out before she lost the nerve.

"You what?" he snickered.

She came over to him. "You probably think I'm foul 'cause I'm doin' this to KG and he my baby father... but I really do have feelings for you. You ain't like all these nigguhs out here... you different. Just give me the chance to show you I'm different, too," she vowed, never losing eye contact. Nikki felt that by being willing to commit an act of murder with him, it was the ultimate show of loyalty. Drama would see she was a down ass chick and take her under his wing.

Shameeq pulled her close then kissed her forehead, nose and lips. "So you want Drama in your life like that, Boo?"

Nikki smiled seductively and bit her bottom lip. "And other places, too," she replied, grabbing his dick.

Shameeq eyed her body thinking about a quickie, but one glance out the window killed that thought.

"He here."

Nikki looked. KG was driving his old Black '88 Seville with the beige rag. She looked up at Shameeq questioningly.

"Just chill," he told her, eyes trained on the car.

They could vaguely hear him blowing the horn repeatedly and the faint thump of his system.

"He's not comin up," she surmised.

Shameeq stayed vigilant.

KG blew the horn several more times then began to pull off. Nikki was about to breathe easy thinking he was leaving, but KG made a U-turn and parked across the street. He hopped out

15

and crossed the street. He kept his head on swivel, looking both ways back and forth, because he was looking for more than cars. He kept his hand tucked under his Avirex coat as he disappeared inside the building.

Nikki's knees got weak knowing what was about to go down. Shameeq peeped her expression so he cupped her chin in his hand and said, "Everything is cool, ok? I got you."

Nikki nodded.

"You wit' me now. Walk like a champion." He winked.

Nikki's eyes lit up with her smile. "I'm good, baby," she assured him, although her stomach was in knots.

"When you let him in... turn your back and walk over to the couch, ai-ight? I'll take care of the rest."

Shameeq went and got in the closet by the door. Nikki stood in the middle of the room hoping it would all be over soon. The knock on the door made her jump!

"Nikki! Open the fuckin' door!" KG demanded.

She took a deep breath, drawing her last ounce of sass then barked, "Boy, wait! Knockin' on the door like you the police!" She unlocked all the locks and opened the door. She turned and walked to the couch like Shameeq had instructed her. "Just let me get my coat!"

"Didn't I tell you be downstairs?!" KG fumed. He felt safer now that he was in her apartment.

KG came deeper into the apartment, allowing Shameeq to ease out of the closet and put the gun to the back of KG's head.

"What up, B? Remember me?" Shameeq hissed like a cobra ready to strike.

KG froze up and damn near shit a brick. "Sha?" he gulped, in a voice so high pitched he sounded like a mouse.
He held his hands where Shameeq could see them.

Shameeq reached around and took the pistol off his waist then he spun KG around to face him.

"Surprise, nigguh." Shameeq smirked.

"Man, my word, I got yo' money!" KG confessed.

"Keep that shit duke, this about that shit last night!"

"What sh—" KG began, but Shameeq smacked the shit out of him with his own gun. KG fell flat on his back while Shameeq continued to pistol whip him.

"Muhfucka you tried to body me?! Huh?! Bitch ass nigguh you missed!" Shameeq huffed then put the gun to his forehead.

"Sha, I swear I don't know what you talkin' about," KG lied, his whole mouth swollen and several teeth lost on the floor.

"I'ma ask you one time and one time only, B... do you want to live?"

KG nodded vigorously.

"Where the other muhfucka? I bodied one of them faggots but I want 'em both or word is bond, I'll body you here and now," Shameeq gritted, cocking back the hammer.
KG quickly weighed his options. Any hope of survival was enough for a coward, because a spineless nigguh can fit in the smallest places.

"You tell me K and I'll give you a pass, because a dead nigguh can't pay me my paper. But if you lie...,"

"Shameeq, he a cat from Grafton Avenue. Cat named Hameef. He 'posed to beep me so I can give him his money," KG blurted out.

"What code he usin?"

"1-1-1."

Dutch

Hailing from Newark, New Jersey, Kwame Teague is the award winning, critically acclaimed, and Essence #1 bestselling author of the street classic Dutch trilogy. His other novels include *The Adventures of Ghetto Sam, The Glory of My Demise, Thug Politics, and Dynasty under the Pseudonym Dutch.*

myspace.com/kwamefreedom
facebook.com/authordutch
twitter.com/kwameakadutch

Coming Soon!

Prelude

"They done let the wrong motherfucker out of HELL!" I snickered, as I exited D.C. Jail with a second chance at life.

Six months ago, I was sitting in a United States Penitentiary in Marion, Illinois trying to beat the sweltering heat, and just reaching a decade on a 46 year-to-LIFE prison term for catching a homicide, and an armed robbery beef.

Fortunately, this time my appeals got my convictions overturned on a legal technicality, and I damn sure wasn't about to go to trial for a second time, once I learned that the same hot motherfuckers were willing to come to court, and sing like a canary again! Instead, I took a 10-to-25 year Manslaughter plea agreement, and walked with time served, because the judge suspended all but ten years that I had served.

With my newfound freedom, I had a purpose to serve. There would be no more hustling for peanuts, and expensive designer clothes; It's a damn shame that I have to quit hustling, but some things more important had to be handled for the forgotten men on lockdown. I've been through several correctional facilities across America, and there hadn't been one guy that wasn't rotting in prison because of a SNITCH!

I even went to the extent of getting those guys contact information just in case they made it back to the streets before I did.

But as you know, I, Carmelo Glover made it first, and I must keep a vow that I'd made the second after I'd got convicted-BY ANY MEANS... And that was, eliminate every hot motherfucker in the streets that I could.

Like every top-notch killer, I had a plan, and as soon as I get them guns, I would begin executing it. Although this time, things were much riskier, but I loved challenges, and this was the biggest one of my life!

1

Hell, if motherfuckers could lie, snitch, and send good men to prison for EONS, then why I couldn't kill their weak asses, and get street justice and revenge for the forgotten ones?

If you're feeling me, then come, and take a ride with me in THE CITY WHERE IT GOES DOWN AT!!!

COMING SOON

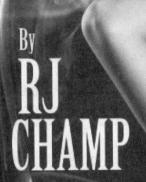

By
RJ
CHAMP

"Beware of DC's charming men... you never know whose path you may cross."

A
BEAUTIFUL
SATAN
A NOVEL

DC BOOKDIVA PUBLICATIONS

PREFACE

The Breaking Point...

The bluish glass window shimmered in the afternoon sun, casting rays of dancing sunlight upon Angel as she slept – warm sunbeams flickering cross her eyelids began to awaken her. Slowly, Angel emerged from sleep. She rolled over in bed, a tired frown etched in her face as long black tresses fell over her eye. Angel felt fuzzy, like she hadn't gotten a wink of sleep.

'What's this?' Her hazel eyes focused now on a crumpled note paper laying on the pillow beside her; the name – NATASHA – scribbled at the top.

The note was a letter from her husband, Rafael.

'Will I ever see you again?' Angel's inner voice wondered as she reflected over the recent loss of Rafael.

"Why, Lord? Why would you allow me to fall in love with a man so deep, then allow Satan to intervene in our lives? Father, you let Satan take my love away. Why??!!" Angel cried out, tears of pain swelling in her eyes.

As if all her energy had just been sucked right out of her, Angel's head collapsed on the pillow. Dazed, Angel stared – spellbound – up at the ceiling, staring of at some distance in the middle of nowhere.

Suddenly the sound of a smooth jazz melody came drifting into the room. Startled, Angel turned and gazed tiredly at the door.

1

'Where's the music coming from?' she silently mused. Shivering, Angel pulled herself to her feet. As she stood, Angel felt a cold chill rise up and through her entire body.

Kenny G's 'Songbird' came floating from the open doorway leading into the master bedroom, as if trying to drown out the pleasurable moans of a woman in some kind of synthetic coup.

Angel lingered in the hallway; a concoction in Whipped-Cream fragranced candles saturated the air outside the master bedroom. Angel's trembling fingers moved along the wall as she reached for the door.

The blonde with crystal-blue eyes, Natasha, was inside the master suite on her hands and knees, doggy-style. She was getting her world rocked by Angel's cheating-ass-husband, Rafael.

Gripping Natasha firmly around her waist, Rafael pounded her insides – pushing al 12-inches of his throbbing organ into the hilt.

"Yea, that's it, bitch," Rafael hissed through clenched teeth. "Who's your daddy now, huh, bitch?" A smug grin spread on his lips – Rafael got off watching Natasha's rump jiggle every time he gave that ass a slap.

Angel stood in the doorway with pure rage simmering in his eyes, grinding her teeth as an icy chill ran down the back of her neck. She let out a scream at the top of her lungs, and then lunged across the room like a woman who had totally lost her mind.

"You dirty-dick-sonofabitch!"

Angel leaped on Rafael's back like a panther with the intent to kill. She hissed, exposing a perfect set of pearly-whites, and sank her sharp teeth deep into the thick-meaty muscle bulging atop Rafael's shoulder.

Sudden shock and fear exploded on Rafael's face. He howled like a wounded wolf and stumbled backward twisting and turning with Angel strapped to his back. It took Rafael all the strength he could summon to pry his crazy wife's arms from around his throat. Rafael spun around and slung Angel toward the bed. His heart dropped instantly and Rafael cringed inside when he realized his mistake.

2

Angel hit the king-size sleigh bed poised on all fours when she landed; she resembled a ferocious feline preparing to attack. Operating on sheer impulse, Angel licked her lips and pounced on the frightened woman. Natasha tried to leap across the bed to escape the clutches of Angel. But Natasha moved to slowly and her attempts at escape were futile.

"Oh no, bitch!" Angel snarled aggressively. "You ain't going nowhere... fucking ho!" Angel grunted, as she tore into Natasha, death gleaming in her eyes. She mounted a vicious assault using fist, teeth, and nails, exerting pain and punishment on Natasha's nude body. The attack was so severe; Natasha swore she was being attacked by more than one woman.

Rafael rushed to Natasha's rescue. "Let her go!" Rafael screamed while locked in a heated struggle – wrestling and tussling to save his battered and bruised lover from the death grip of his enraged wife.

Angel's uncontrollable rage had her adrenaline pumping in overdrive, her strength was uncanny. Rafael had to use all 220-pounds of his muscular frame to lift Angel in the air. He was stretched to the limit, all six feet of Rafael stood erect. Rafael gave one last forceful push breaking the death-hold Angel had on Natasha.

When Angel released her grip, Rafael felt the wind knock out of him from the full impact of Angel's weight crashing on top of him.

Angel bounced to her feet immediately when she realized Rafael was injured. She hovered over him, glaring.

"You like laying with sluts!" she yelled rancorously.

'You dirty-dick-bitch!" Angel cocked her right foot back, aimed for Rafael's dick, and kicked him as hard as she could. With a snide smirk twitching at the corners of her mouth, Angel leaned over Rafael's face, coughed-up a snotty blob of phlegm, and hawk-spit right in his face. "You and your whore can burn in hell!!!"

Moments later, Angel could see herself standing in the doorway just outside the master bathroom staring across the dark interior as if she was having some weird out-of-body experience. Angel could feel an eerie presence radiating from the still dark-

3

ness inside the bathroom like there was some kind of unforeseen and ungodly force lingering in its space. Angel focused straight ahead on the large walled mirror and saw the silhouette framed in the doorway was her own reflection.

Angel took a step inside the bathroom and was surprised at how chilly the air was inside. With caution in her every step, Angel walked to the mirror and gazed at herself. Angel looked discombobulated when she noticed a bright white t-shirt covering her torso. She couldn't remember putting on the shirt. Angel looked down at the white tee, her fingers trembling as they brushed against the wet cotton. NATASHA was finger-painted in fresh blood on the front in large crimson letters. Angel froze, utter horror and disbelief radiating in her expression. Slowly her head rose towards the mirror and Angel's eyes twinkled strangely with an insanity that made her inwardly cringe. An ice cold sensation pierced Angel to the core when she saw the inverted reflection of Natasha's name in the mirror! Spelled in fresh blood, the word 'AH-SATAN" seemed to leap off the shirt. The crude painted letters were all Angel could see. She stared at herself in the looking glass and realized with terror the woman looking back was a total stranger.

Suddenly the fog lifted from Angel's eyes and she was brought back to reality. She realized she was still on the bed, gazing up at the ceiling. Shaken, Angel bolted upright and reached out to yank open the top drawer of the nightstand. She pulled out a prescription pill bottle with the narcotic Oxyline printed on the label.

Angel popped two pills in her mouth, tossed the pill bottle back in the drawer, and then closed her eyes tightly, exhaling deeply…

"Father-God, I pray for you to vanquish the bad dreams, the bad feelings and the bad demons that I feel surrounding me and taunting me. Please, oh Lord, I know that I am nothing without you. So please have mercy on me… I put no other above you. I'm begging you, Lord, please bless me with a real man so I can move forward with my life and forget Raphael. Help me purge my husband's unclean spirit from my soul…Help me Father-God, I need you…please!"

4

COMING SOON

DC BOOKDIVA PRESENTS

TRINA
THE HYDRO KILLER

DARRELL DEBREW

Order Form

DC Bookdiva Publications
#245 4401-A Connecticut Avenue, NW
Washington, DC 20008
dcbookdiva.com

Name: _____

Inmate ID _____

Address: _____

City/State: _____ **Zip:** _____

QUANTITY	TITLES	PRICE	TOTAL
	Up The Way, Ben	15.00	
	Dynasty By Dutch	15.00	
	Dynasty 2 By Dutch	15.00	
	Coming Soon!		
	Trina	15.00	
	A Killer'z Ambition	15.00	
	A Beautiful Satan	15.00	
	The Hustle	15.00	
	Q, Dutch	15.00	

Sub Total $_____

Shipping/Handling (Via US Media Mail) $3.95 1-2 books, $7.95 1-3 Books,
4 or more titles-Free Shipping

Shipping $ _____

Total Enclosed $ _____

FORMS OF ACCEPTED PAYMENTS:
Certified or government issued checks and money orders, all mail in orders take 5-7 Business days to be delivered. Books can also be purchased on our website at dcbookdiva.com and by credit card at 1866-928-9990. Incarcerated readers receive 25% discount. Please pay $11.25 per book and apply the same shipping terms as stated above.

COMING SOON

THE HUSTLE

NOVEL BY
FRAZIER BOY